How Dyslexic Benny Became a Star

A story of hope for dyslexic children and their parents

By Joe Griffith

Yorktown Press
P.O. Box 795667
Dallas, Texas 75379-5667
(972) 233-7130

How Dyslexic Benny Became a Star

A story of hope for dyslexic children and their parents

Published by:

Yorktown Press
P.O. Box 795667
Dallas, TX 75379-5667

10 9 8 7 6 5 4 3 2 1

Publisher's Cataloging-in-Publication
(Provided by Quality Books, Inc.)

Griffith, Joe, 1941-
How dyslexic Benny became a star : a story of hope for dyslexic children and their parents / by Joe Griffith ; [Jenny Schulz, illustrator]. -- 1st ed.
p. cm.
ISBN: 0-9659379-0-9
SUMMARY: A fifth-grade boy with dyslexia decides to join the school's football team.

1. Dyslexia—Juvenile fiction. 2. Football for children--Juvenile fiction. I. Title.

PZ7.G75Ho 1997 [Fic]
QBI97-40987

What Experienced Educators Say . . .

"Let's hope that all teachers and their students will read about Benny. Children with dyslexia will see some of themselves in Benny, and other children will become more aware of what dyslexia really is."

Marcia K. Henry, Ph.D., Past President
The International Dyslexia Society

"You managed to capture the feelings of pain and embarrassment children with dyslexia experience both in and out of school, as well as the feelings of hope and joy that come with finding someone who understands. I can't wait to share it with some children I know who are struggling just as Benny did."

Nell Carvell, Past President
Academic Language Therapist Assn. (ALTA)

"WOW! Your story is wonderful."

Connie Burkhaulter, M.Ed., C.A.L.T.
Education Coordinator
Scottish Rite Hospital for Children

"You are to be congratulated on writing an interesting, thought-provoking story that educates. The reaction of Benny's friends, teachers, and parents are typical and the behavior Benny develops is characteristic."

Joyce S. Pickering, Executive Director
Shelton School & Evaluation Center

"*How Dyslexic Benny Became a Star* was especially heart warming, because we really need to hear happy endings."

Beverly Dooley, Ph.D., Executive Director
Southwest Multisensory Training Center

"I feel that your book will help ease the pain and the misgivings both child and parent have about our special gift."

Dianne Throgmartin, President
The Dyslexic Educational Foundation of America

"Great book! My students hung on every word. They were so encouraged by the end."

Kay Peterson, Academic Language Therapist

"As a parent of a dyslexic child, I could relate to the story on a personal basis and must admit it brought tears to my eyes."

Connie Lewis, Parent

"As a librarian, I can't wait to see this book in the library. It will appeal to many readers."

Sharyn Larson, Librarian

What the Children Say . . .

"It's the <u>best</u> book that any teacher has ever read to me.

I liked the book because Benny is just like me. It will encourage dyslexics and let them know that people care."

Diana

"I thought your story about Benny was terrific. It will encourage many dyslexic kids and adults not to ever stop putting in effort. It is a great example to everyone."

Tammie

"Your book taught a great lesson. The next time someone wants to make fun of another person they'll think about what they read and they won't do it. That is what makes the book so special."

Brent

"Your book is better than any book I have ever read. I like the story because Benny went through a lot but he didn't give up."

Latoya

"I loved your story. It was wonderful because it told us not to make fun of people that can not read right."

Kelly

"I liked your story because it tells that you can do whatever you want when you put yourself to it."

Sabrina

"If more people would read this book they would stop making fun of other dyslexic people."

Brandon

"I learned that I am not the only one who has a problem. It tells me even though I'm not good at something I should always do my best."

Whitney

"The story you wrote was so great I can't get it out of my mind."

Estefana

"I liked your story because teachers can learn that some students are getting taught the wrong way."

Natasha

"Because I am dyslexic I know what Benny was going through because people call me stupid and they make fun of me because I am in language training. The story made me feel better because I think I can do anything that I want to do."

Jessica

"I really like your book because now I know that I am not the only one that is dyslexic in this world."

Jacob

"I learned that it's okay to be dyslexic and not to feel bad because I am smart."

Rachael

"Your book was an inspiration for me. I'm not a dyslexic but it was still inspiring to me and my friends."

Lisa

"I really liked your book. It was neat how Benny was stupid then became a star."

Justin

How Dyslexic Benny Became a Star
is available on audio cassettes.

To order from your bookstore ask for
ISBN # 09659379-1-7.

For direct orders of the book and tape use our Web page at www.yorktownpress.com.

Foreword

How Dyslexic Benny Became a Star is a touching account of one youngster's struggle in learning to read and the painful journey that he took to gain self-confidence, self-respect, and tremendous success as a human being, as a student, and as an athlete. Few people understand the agony of dyslexia and the wrenching effects that not being able to read, write, and spell have on the developing child and his family. Most individuals take learning how to read for granted because for many the path to reading mastery and the knowledge that reading makes accessible is unencumbered and devoid of the frustration, fear, and embarrassment that are constant companions of the dyslexic. But try and put yourself in the shoes of a child who meets with failure every time he attempts to read, and how he must feel when his failure is so visible to those around him. As Joe Griffith has taught us so well in this book, being bright and talented in many areas is a double-edged sword for Benny and for many with dyslexia. The same intelligence and brightness that provides dyslexics with outstanding conceptual and problem-solving skills in areas other than reading, also intensifies their own perceptions of how they differ from their peers. For Benny, this was clearly the case, and his ability to reflect on his own difficulties made him feel stupid and worthless.

But Joe Griffith has taught us how sensitive parents and teachers can figuratively save the life of a youngster like Benny by making sure that his talents are recognized and brought to the fore so they can flourish and serve as the foundation for self-concept and self-esteem. The fact that Benny's life can now be described as a success story is indeed a tribute to his Mom, Dad, his teachers, but mostly to Benny. His early pain gave him the strength and courage to pursue his dreams, and Joe Griffith has painted us a poignant picture of how Benny traveled the hard road to achieve those dreams. Benny's story stands as a tribute to the human spirit and should serve as an excellent resource for students with dyslexia, their parents, and their teachers.

G. Reid Lyon, Ph.D.
The National Institute of Child Health and Human Development
The National Institutes of Health

Acknowledgment

It took a lot of help from others to put this book into your hands. When I first came up with the idea of writing a story of hope for dyslexic children my first stop was my old friend Beverly Dooley. She convinced me that dyslexic children needed an inspiring book that had a happy ending.

Gladys Kolenovsky, Martha Sibley, and Connie Burkhalter are very busy, but they still graciously answered all of my questions.

Kathy Pomara helped me settle on a story idea.

Bill Sloan, whose talent knows no bounds, did a superb job of editing.

Four dedicated teachers—Kay Peterson, Becky Griffith, Amy Phillips, and Connie Lewis—gladly tested the impact of Benny's story by reading it to their fourth- and fifth-grade classes. Some of the students' letters are included in the first part of the book.

Many others deserve special thanks: Sharyn Larson, Julie Williams, Jo Ann Horton, and Rickie Searle.

About The Author

Because of dyslexia, Joe Griffith never read a book until he was 22 years old, but now he has had three books published.

Joe has also been a movie actor, comedian, commercial pilot, real estate developer, stockbroker, and a co-host of America's first-ever business television show.

In 1971 he became a motivational speaker. Since then he has spoken 3,000 times before some of the world's most prestigious audiences. But one speech stands out like no other. He spoke to a school for dyslexic boys and girls. For the first time, Joe stepped away from the corporate world and revealed the painful side of his life. Afterwards, kids stood in line asking Joe questions that begged for encouragement.

Overcome by the experience, Joe promised that someday he'd help these kids reduce their sense of hopelessness, a feeling Joe had often experienced too. He combined his 26 years as a motivational speaker and his personal struggle with dyslexia to write ***How Dyslexic Benny Became a Star***, a powerful story that offers hope to dyslexic children and their parents.

Other Books by Joe Griffith

How The Platform Professionals Keep 'Em Laughin' **(Rich Publishing)**

Speaker's Library of Business Stories, Anecdotes & Humor **(Prentice Hall)**

Dedication

To all the loving people who have unselfishly dedicated themselves to helping dyslexic children.

Chapter 1

Benny's Big Chance

Benny was having more trouble than usual concentrating in class this afternoon. It was the second day of a brand-new school term, but he was too distracted to think about English or math. He wasn't even worried about somebody calling him "Stupid Benny" again. The only thing on his mind right now was his after-school meeting with Coach Watkins.

Yesterday the coach had announced that he needed as many fifth- and sixth-grade boys as he could get for the Wheeler Elementary football team. When the message came over the school's public address system, Benny's eyes had lit up. It was as if the coach had been talking only to him.

Benny was starting fifth grade now, and feeling "stupid" in class had become a way of life for him. But he was sure he could be a good football player if he got the chance. He could run really fast, and he spent many hours each week throwing and catching a football all by himself. It would have been more fun to have some friends to play with, but the other boys in the neighborhood didn't hang around Benny much anymore. Over the past two or three years, he had become a "loner."

Everything had been OK when he was in first grade. Nobody knew then how much trouble Benny was going to have with his reading. But in second grade, whenever his teacher asked him to read aloud, he always got the words mixed up.

"No, Benny, that word isn't <u>saw</u>; it's <u>was</u>," the teacher would say.

Soon his classmates started snickering at his repeated mistakes. In third grade, the snickering increased. And in fourth grade, it just got worse and worse. Finally, the snickers turned into loud laughter. Even the girls started joining in.

Toward the end of last year, the principal asked Benny's mom and dad to come to his office. He told them that Benny had fallen too far behind the rest of his class. "If he doesn't start reading better, we may have to hold him back," the principal said.

After that, even Benny's parents seemed irritated and impatient with him. His mother fussed and fretted and called him her "little boy." He could tell by the sound of her voice that she was disappointed in him. But Benny's father took the news even worse. He acted as if Benny's problems at school were an insult to the family's good name.

"Benny isn't stupid," his father said angrily. "He's just lazy, that's all."

Somehow, Benny managed to move up to fifth grade with the rest of his class. As the new term approached, he promised himself he'd do better this time. But by now, his promises had an empty, defeated sound. He promised to do better every year. The problem was he never did.

When he thought about Coach Watkins' announcement yesterday, Benny's heart thumped with excitement. When the last class bell rang, he didn't leave the building through the front door. He was so eager to get to see the coach that he jumped out the classroom window.

Benny was so eager to get to see the coach that he jumped out the classroom window.

He ran to the practice field as hard as he could run. But when he saw that no one was there but Coach Watkins, Benny felt a little scared. He decided to hide behind a trash dumpster until more kids arrived. He didn't want to have to talk to the coach by himself. The coach might ask him questions, and that would make Benny nervous. He got more questions than he could handle in class.

Benny hid behind the dumpster until most of the other boys showed up. Then he slipped quietly onto the field and joined the group that had formed around Coach Watkins. At first, Benny stayed in the background. He didn't want the coach to single him out or call attention to him. If the coach did that, Benny knew he would probably do something silly—just as he did in class when the teacher called on him to read.

For the past year, Benny had acted silly a lot. If the other kids were going to laugh at him anyway, he decided to be the "class clown." Then he could tell himself he was making them laugh on purpose. That way, it wasn't so embarrassing when he couldn't read. And if he acted silly and unruly enough, the teacher would skip over Benny and call on someone else.

It had happened again just this morning when Mrs. Blocker, his new teacher, called on him. "Benny, would you read the next page please?" she asked.

Benny felt tense and panicky, but he hid his feelings behind a silly grin. "WHY NOT?" he yelled as loud as he could.

His yell startled Mrs. Blocker, and she jumped as if she had heard a shot. Several of Benny's classmates giggled.

"Cut that out, Benny," Mrs. Blocker said. "Now read the next page."

"WHY NOT?" he bellowed again. This time, the whole classroom burst out laughing.

Mrs. Blocker just shook her head and turned away from Benny. "John, will you read for me please?" she said quietly to the boy at the next desk.

Mrs. Blocker didn't call on Benny again all day. She had avoided him the same way his fourth-grade teacher had done last year. But that didn't keep him from feeling "stupid." Actually, it only made him feel more stupid. It was only the second day of school and he was already off to a terrible start.

But maybe if he could be a good football player, it would make up for all his failures in class, Benny thought. He sat on the ground with the other boys, gazing admiringly at Coach Watkins. The coach was marching back and forth before the group of thirty boys like a general reviewing his troops. He wore a gray sweatsuit and had a silver whistle dangling around his neck.

The coach was marching before the group of boys like a general reviewing his troops.

"OK, guys, we're out here to win football games for Wheeler Elementary," the coach told them. "If you want to help us do that, then I want you on my team. I need linemen to block and receivers to catch the ball. I need a quarterback to call the signals and running backs to run. I need linebackers and cornerbacks and safeties to tackle and break up passes."

Benny listened intently to every word Coach Watkins said. In his heart, Benny knew the football field was one place he could succeed. Making the team would make him happier than he had ever been. He didn't know or care how the other boys sitting around him felt about it. Benny was determined to play football, no matter what.

"I'll show them," Benny told himself. "I'll show everybody. Then they'll never call me 'Stupid Benny' again!"

Chapter 2

Benny Gets Permission

After the meeting with Coach Watkins, Benny hurried home. Tomorrow would be the first day of real practice, and he couldn't wait to tell his mom and dad that he was going to be a football player. He burst through the front door and ran to show his mother the permission slip that Coach Watkins had given him.

"Mom, Mom, you've got to sign this," he shouted. "I want to play football!"

His mother frowned as she looked at the permission slip. "Just calm down," she said. "We'll talk to your dad about it when he gets home."

That night, Benny was glad his sister Maggie was having dinner at a friend's house. Maggie was two years older than Benny, and she seemed to enjoy picking on him. If she was there, Benny knew she'd say something about how stupid he was and do her best to ruin his chances of playing football.

Benny and his parents were at the dinner table when his mom told his dad about the football permission slip. Benny was so tense he could hardly eat, but his dad's reaction came as a pleasant surprise.

"Sure, I think that's a great idea," his dad said. "I played football when I was your age, Benny, and I liked it a lot. It'll be a good experience for you."

"But what if Benny gets hurt?" his mom said uneasily.

"He'll be just fine," his dad said. "It'll help toughen him up and make a man out of him."

"But what about his classwork?" his mother said. "I don't see how playing football is going to help his grades."

"Oh, just stop worrying about that," his dad said, raising his voice a little. "Benny needs to learn about teamwork and meeting challenges. Besides, maybe football will help him make some friends. I think it could be the best thing in the world for him."

Benny could hardly believe his ears. For once, his dad was actually on his side. It was hard to remember the last time that had happened. Sometimes it seemed as if his dad had done nothing but fuss at him ever since Benny's first report card in first grade.

The argument between his parents was nothing new to Benny. They seemed to argue a lot, and most of the time Benny seemed to be the cause of their disagreements. Sometimes he could hear them arguing long after they thought he was asleep.

"Benny needs special help in school, Larry," his mother would say. "He has some kind of a learning problem, especially in reading."

"I'm telling you, Kathy, there's nothing wrong with Benny except laziness," his father would reply. "He's just as smart as the other kids. All he needs to do is work a little harder."

Benny finished his dinner and excused himself. He knew his dad would convince his mom to let him play football. His dad always seemed to win their arguments. And if Benny was going to be a star player, he needed to start getting ready for tomorrow's practice. He grabbed his football and headed for the backyard.

Benny had made up his mind that afternoon that he wanted to play quarterback. To do that, he needed to be a really good passer. He spent the next hour alone in the backyard, throwing the ball to imaginary receivers who scored a touchdown every time.

It would have been nice to have a real person to catch the ball for a change. But once he was a star, Benny thought, things would be different. When he was the star quarterback of the Wheeler Elementary Tigers, he wouldn't have any trouble finding other kids to play with. Everybody would want to play with him then. People would applaud him, not laugh at him.

Chapter 3

Benny's First Football Practice

The next afternoon, Benny was again the first kid to reach the practice field, but this time he wasn't nearly as scared. For some reason he couldn't explain, he thought he could trust Coach Watkins to treat him fairly. At least he hoped so. That was more than he could expect from any of his other teachers.

"What's your name?" Coach Watkins asked.

"Benny Whitley," said Benny.

"Are you excited about playing football?"

"Yes sir," Benny said. "I've never been this excited before. I want to play quarterback, coach."

Coach Watkins smiled. "Well, we'll see how it goes," he said. "Just remember, there are twenty-two different positions on the team, and each one's important."

After all the players arrived, the coach told them to line up on the goal line and get ready to run some sprints. "I'll stand out here at midfield," he said. "And when I blow my whistle, you run past me."

The whistle blew, and all the boys took off. As they gained speed, Benny was one of the frontrunners. Some of the boys who were overweight or out of shape finished five or ten yards behind the others, but everybody made it. Benny was the third player to cross the fifty-yard line, but he had the feeling he could do better.

"OK, guys," said Coach Watkins. "Now we're going to line up on the fifty-yard line and run back to the end zone."

He blew the whistle again, and the boys raced toward the goal line. After two more sprints, the whole group was panting like a bunch of tired hunting dogs—except for Benny. On the last run, he crossed the finish line first.

"Good sprints, boys," the coach said, grinning straight at Benny. "Now it's time to get your uniforms and get suited up."

Tired but eager to put on their first-ever uniform, the players followed the coach into the locker room. For thirty minutes, they sorted through the maze of green and white uniforms. Finally, each boy found one that fit—or at least almost fit. Then the uniformed players trotted back outside with renewed energy.

Coach Watkins pulled a wrinkled sheet of paper out of his pocket and unfolded it. "All right," he said. "I'm going to read off your name and the positions you're going to be trying out for, so listen up!"

A few minutes later, when he shouted out, "Benny Whitley, quarterback," some of the other guys made faces and groaned. A few laughed and poked each other in the ribs. Someone snickered, "Stupid Benny a quarterback? What a joke! He can't even read." Benny tried to ignore them. He knew they thought he wouldn't be able to remember the plays. And even if he did, they thought he'd probably call them out wrong.

But he would show them, Benny told himself fiercely. He'd be the best quarterback that Wheeler Elementary ever had. He'd prove he wasn't "Stupid Benny" anymore, no matter what they thought.

Chapter 4

Benny Still Has to Study

All week long, Benny was the first boy at practice and the last to leave. The first time he got tackled, it hurt a little, but he quickly shook it off. The pain wasn't nearly as bad as the pain he had felt a hundred times in class. And when he threw a touchdown pass in the big game on Saturday, it would be worth a few bumps and bruises. Nobody would ever laugh at him again after that. They'd be too busy cheering.

But each day in the classroom, Benny's same old problems just went on and on. The teachers didn't care that he was a budding football star. They kept right on correcting him when he said read instead of dead or run when the word was gun. They also let him know that if he didn't make his grades, he couldn't play football. The school had a stupid rule called "no pass, no play."

The thought of being dropped from the team for bad grades made Benny feel sick and shaky inside. Every night, he sat at the kitchen table with his mother while she drilled him on spelling words and multiplication tables.

"What's six times six?" she asked on Wednesday.

"Uh, sixty-four," Benny guessed.

"No, Benny. Think about it and try again."

"What's six times six?" Benny's mom asked.

Benny wished he could quit school and play football full time. "Forty-four?" he said hopefully.

His Mom rolled her eyes and shook her head. "Six times six is thirty-six, Benny," she said. "Now say that back to me. Keep saying it until I tell you to stop."

"Six times six is thirty-six. Six times six is thirty-six. Six times six is . . ."

During his tutoring sessions, Benny's sister often found some reason to come through the kitchen.

"I don't see why you're helping him, Mom," Maggie said. "Benny doesn't even try at school."

"That's a lie!" he cried. "I DO try at school."

He felt like throwing his math book at his sister. She was always calling him names like "Benny the Dip" and "my weird brother." Benny didn't know that all older sisters thought their younger brothers were dippy and weird.

"Stop it, both of you," their mother said. "Just get what you need, Maggie, and go back to your room."

Benny and his mom studied for another half-hour before she gave up for the night. Then he went into the den where his dad was watching TV and sat down on the couch. There was a talk show on the screen about fat people who had a hard time losing weight. One man was complaining about how awful it was to weigh 420 pounds.

"You just think you've got problems," Benny thought. "I'd trade mine for yours any day."

Chapter 5

Coach Watkins Likes Benny

Jack Watkins had been coaching at Wheeler Elementary for five years, and this year's team looked to be his best yet. He had some big, husky kids for offensive and defensive lines, and several of his players showed real athletic talent. But the most important thing was that they all seemed enthusiastic—especially Benny Whitley.

The coach had thought about Benny a lot over the past week or so. He had heard that the kid had some kind of problem in school, and that the other boys often made fun of him. In a way, Benny reminded Jack Watkins of himself when he was Benny's age, but he still wasn't sure just what Benny's problem was.

The coach couldn't help but wonder if he'd made a mistake putting Benny at quarterback. Benny was a good athlete and one of the fastest players on the team. But the coach just wasn't sure the quarterback position was a good fit for Benny. A successful quarterback had to think fast, stay cool, and be a team leader. He had to be able to inspire his teammates.

But before Benny could inspire others, he would have to boost his own self-confidence. That was why Jack Watkins had decided to give the kid a shot at playing quarterback. If it turned out that the coach was wrong, he could always move Benny to another position.

"Tomorrow's the big day, boys," Coach Watkins told the team on Friday. "We play our first game of the season against cross-town rival Chester Elementary, and we're going to have our hands full. Chester was runner-up for the city trophy last year, and I hear they're pretty good again. The game starts at 2 p.m., and everybody needs to be here and suited up by 1:30. Go get 'em, Tigers!"

The kids all yelled and cheered, and some of them waved their fists in the air.

"Remember," the coach said. "We want to bring that city trophy back to Wheeler Elementary. It's been a long time since we won it, but I know we can do it this year!"

As the players ran off the field, most of them were laughing and doing "high-fives" with each other. But Coach Watkins noticed that Benny wasn't even smiling. There was a look of grim determination on his face.

Chapter 6

Benny's Big Game

Benny was so excited about tomorrow's game that he wore his football uniform to bed, shoulder pads and all. But his excitement couldn't stop the worries and doubts that tugged at his mind.

He had the same fluttery feelings in his stomach as he did when he faced a reading test. And he felt the same old fear of choosing the wrong answer or doing the wrong thing. As he stared intently at the dark ceiling of his room, he could almost see the words "stupid" and "lazy" dancing around like flashes of lightning.

Benny knew he should have been thrilled about playing in his first football game. But the threat of failure hung over him like a sword. Long after his parents had turned out the lights and gone to sleep, Benny lay there wide awake.

Saturday was warm and sunny—a beautiful September day. Benny rode to the game with his parents. He sat in the back seat of the family van with his sister and tried to ignore her teasing remarks. She kept telling him how goofy he looked in his uniform. "Your pants are too loose," she laughed.

When they got to the football field, Benny saw Miss Crabtree, his teacher from last year, sitting in the third row of the bleachers. She had made him feel like a fool a thousand times during fourth grade. Benny knew she saw him, but she didn't smile. "Oh, well," he told himself, "she may know a lot about reading and math, but she can't play quarterback." The thought made him feel a little better, and he forced himself to turn and wave at her as he trotted past.

The Wheeler Tigers assembled at the north end of the field for warmup drills. At the opposite end of the field, they could see their opponents doing the same thing. The Chester players wore blue jerseys with white numbers. The Tigers' uniforms were white with green numbers.

Suddenly, it was time for the game to start. Wheeler won the coin toss and elected to receive the kickoff. "Everybody gather around," Coach Watkins said. "If we're going to win that city trophy, we have to start today. That means we all have to play as hard as we can and never give up. Remember, we're a team. We all win together."

All the players clapped their hands and the starters moved out onto the field to take up their positions.

Chester's kickoff was short and bouncing. Richie Hawkins, one of Wheeler's bigger linemen, grabbed the ball, and eleven blue jerseys immediately piled on top of him.

Coach Watkins started Tim Davis at quarterback, but he told Benny not to worry. "You'll get plenty of playing time. Just be patient."

That was easier said than done, though. Benny paced the sideline anxiously, staying close to the coach and hoping after every play that he would get to go into the game. There was no way he could be patient, he thought, when he had so much to prove. He had to prove that everybody was wrong about "Stupid Benny." He had to get out there and show them all!

The time ticked rapidly off the clock, and the first quarter ended in a scoreless tie. Benny was starting to feel desperate. He even caught himself hoping Tim Davis would get hurt. Then the coach would have to send Benny in, and Benny would win the game—he knew he would! He also knew it was wrong to want someone else to be injured, but he couldn't help himself.

For three quarters, Wheeler and Chester battled each other to a 0-0 tie. Neither team was able to move the ball very well. The Tigers had made only four first downs, and Tim Davis had completed only one pass. But Coach Watkins still hadn't pulled Tim from the lineup, and Benny was beginning to wonder if he ever would.

The fourth quarter was nearly half gone when the Tigers had to punt the ball away again. Finally, the coach turned to Benny and put his arm around his shoulders.

"I'm sending you in as soon as we get the ball back, Benny," Coach Watkins whispered. "Tim's done a good job, but he's tired, and I think a fresh quarterback can win the game for us."

"I can do it, Coach," Benny promised. His heart was pounding like a hammer in his chest.

He wished he felt as sure of himself as he sounded.

"I know you can," the coach assured him. "On the first two plays, I want you to hand off to Billy Turner and let him run the ball to the right side." The coach opened his play book and showed Benny a sheet of paper with the number and diagram of a play drawn on it. "Then, on the third play, this is what I want you to do. Even if Billy picks up a first down, you run this play the third time the ball is snapped. I've already talked to the other guys about it, and they'll all be ready for it. Understand?"

Benny hardly looked at the diagram of the play, but he stared at the number and read it silently to himself. It looked like "81-L-P." He closed his eyes and concentrated as hard as he could. Now he remembered. It was a pass play to the left to number 81, Ronnie Acres, the tight end. They had practiced it a dozen times that week.

"Do you know the play, Benny?" the coach asked. "Are you sure you remember what to do?"

Benny nodded. "Yeah, Coach, I remember," he said, hoping he could really do it.

Chester made three straight first downs, but the drive stalled near midfield and they had to punt. Wheeler returned the kick all the way to the Chester thirty-five-yard line, giving the Tigers good field position. But by this time, less than three and a half minutes remained on the clock. Time was running out for Benny and his teammates.

"81-L-P," Benny repeated to himself as he joined the huddle. "81-L-P. 81-L-P." He couldn't let himself forget. He couldn't afford to mess up. He had to do it right. He had to!

Then Benny was bending down behind the center. "Hut, one! Hut, two!" he barked, but he barely heard his own voice calling the signals because his heart was beating so loud.

Billy Turner ran for a three-yard gain the first time Benny handed him the ball. But on the next play, Billy was stopped right at the line of scrimmage. Third down was coming up. It was the biggest moment of Benny's life as he called the play in the huddle. He was about to throw the game-winning pass. He was about to be a star! The number of the play the coach had shown him glowed like a neon sign in his brain.

81-L-P. 81-L-P.

As Benny walked up to the line, his hands were trembling. It was almost the same as when a teacher called on him to read aloud. But he gritted his teeth and yelled out the signals. The ball shot into his hands and he took five quick steps backward, looking down the field for the tall figure of Ronnie Acres and his big green number 81.

But something was wrong. Ronnie was nowhere in sight. In fact, nobody was running a pass route. Instead everybody was blocking along the line. Benny didn't understand what was happening.

He dashed frantically to his left to escape a tackler. He still couldn't find Ronnie Acres, but Benny saw his other receiver ten yards downfield, right between two defensive backs. Somehow he had to get the ball to him. Benny was almost to the sideline and two more tacklers were closing in.

He reared back and threw the ball as hard as he could in the direction of his man downfield. But instead of zipping sharply through the air like he wanted it to, the ball came out of his hand wrong and fluttered like a wounded duck. The receiver acted as if he never even saw it coming, but one of the Chester defenders was right there waiting for it.

Benny watched in horror as the figure in the blue jersey reached up and intercepted the pass. Then the Chester defender was hugging the

Benny watched in horror as his pass was intercepted.

ball and racing down the sideline. He was running past the stunned Wheeler team and heading straight for the Tigers' end zone.

Benny made a desperate lunge as the guy darted past him, but he was just out of reach. With Benny sprawled helplessly on the turf, the Chester player scored the winning touchdown just as the clock ran out.

The visitors' section of the stands exploded into wild cheers and shouting. The whole Chester team swarmed the little cornerback who had made the interception. They all fell in a pile on the ground, hugging and yelling and pounding each other.

Wheeler's fans sat in stunned disbelief. The Tiger players yanked off their helmets and slammed them down in disgust. Then they walked slowly off the field with their heads down.

Benny sat alone on the thirty-yard line, wishing he could disappear or die—or both. He kept his helmet on to hide the tears that ran down his cheeks. Out of the corner of his eye, he saw Coach Watkins standing on the sideline shaking his head.

Of all the agonizing moments Benny had endured, this was the worst. No classroom failure or flunked test had ever left him so totally crushed, so utterly defeated.

Everybody had known the truth about him from the beginning. His teachers, his principal, his parents, his sister, his teammates—they had all been right. He WAS stupid, he WAS "Stupid Benny," and that was all he would ever be. Why had he ever thought he could be anything else?

He was completely worthless—the same big zero he had always been. The only difference was that now they'd all hate him more than ever. And they had every reason to hate him. He deserved it.

Benny's heart was no longer pounding, but he could still hear its dull thud in his ears. "Duh-stupid! Duh-stupid! Duh-stupid!" it seemed to be saying.

He was lying in the grass along the sideline, never wanting to go home or face his parents when he heard soft footsteps beside him. He looked up and saw Coach Watkins standing over him.

To Benny's amazement, the coach was smiling. It wasn't exactly a happy smile, but it WAS a smile. He sat down on the ground a couple of feet away and wrapped his arms around his knees. When he spoke, there was no anger in his voice.

"Benny, I don't want you to feel bad about what happened today," he said. "You did the best you could, and it just didn't work out. Sometimes things happen that way. We all have to learn from our mistakes. And sometimes messing up helps us do better next time."

Benny tried not to start crying again, but he couldn't help it. "I'll never do better," he said. "And there won't be a next time. I'm a jerk, and I don't belong here. I don't belong anywhere."

"Sit up, Benny," the coach said quietly. "You and I need to talk."

Benny pulled off his helmet and swiped at the tears on his face. "What's there to talk about?" he demanded.

"For one thing, I know how you feel."

"No, you don't," Benny flared. "You're not the one who lost the game. You're not the one who gets blamed. Nobody knows how I feel. And nobody cares, either."

"That's not true," the coach said. "I do know how you feel. I also know we lost today because of me. It was my fault, not yours."

Benny swiped at the tears on his face.

Benny looked up, wondering if he had misunderstood what the coach said. "Because of YOU?" he said. "What do you mean?"

"I put you in the wrong position, Benny," Coach Watkins said. "You're the fastest man on our team. With your speed, you need to be playing defensive back. There's not a receiver on any of the teams we play that you couldn't cover like a blanket."

"Well, it doesn't matter," Benny said. "I'm quitting the team. I don't ever want to play football again. I'm just no good."

"Who says you're no good?"

"Everybody. My teachers, the other kids. Even my dad."

The coach looked squarely into Benny's eyes. "They're wrong, Ben," he said. "And quitting's not going to solve anything. You'd only feel worse if you quit. Besides, it wouldn't be fair to the team. If we're going to win that city trophy, we need you at cornerback."

"The other guys don't want me on the team," Benny said. "Not after today."

"They will when they see you at cornerback," the coach said. "Look, you were out of position today, that's all. Give me a chance to make up for my mistake. Come back and try it at cornerback—just for a week. What do you say, Ben?"

Benny studied the coach's face. He could never remember anyone calling him "Ben" before. It made him feel, well, more important somehow. It had a more grown-up sound to it than "Benny."

"Well . . ." he said. "I'll give it a try."

"You won't be sorry," the coach said. He grinned and put his arm around Benny's shoulder, the way he had done just before he sent him into the game.

"So long, Coach," Benny said. He turned slowly toward the van where his sister and parents were waiting, dreading what they were going to say. He wished he could just stay there in the grass for the rest of the weekend.

"Say, Ben," the coach called after him. "Tell me one more thing before you go, will you?"

"Sure, what do you want to know?"

"Just exactly what play were you running when the ball got intercepted?"

Benny looked puzzled. "It was the one you told me to run, Coach," he said. "You know, 81-L-P. What about it?"

For just a second, a look of surprise crossed the coach's face. Then a light seemed to dawn in his eyes, and he shrugged. "Oh, uh, I was just curious," he said. "It's no big deal. See you at practice on Monday, Ben."

After Benny had left, Jack Watkins picked up his play book from the bench. He turned to the sheet of paper he had shown Benny on the sideline. He looked at the number at the top of the sheet for a long time. The number was "18-L-D," not "81-L-P" as Benny had read it.

"18-L-D" was a quarterback draw, which meant the quarterback was supposed to keep the ball and run with it. Everyone else was supposed to block—even the tight end and the wide receiver. The coach had hoped to fool the Chester team and take advantage of Benny's superior speed to score a touchdown. But "81-L-P," the play Benny had actually run, was a pass to the tight end.

No wonder it hadn't worked, the coach thought. Now he understood. The fact that Benny had misread the number of the play explained a lot of things.

And it also told Jack Watkins more about Benny Whitley—and Benny's problems in school—than he had ever known before.

Chapter 7

Benny Gets a Second Chance

The next week wasn't an easy one for Benny. It couldn't have started off much worse. In the halls at school on Monday morning, many of the other students pointed and laughed and whispered to each other when Benny walked past. And his performance in class was just as bad as ever. In fact, the only bright spots of the whole week were at football practice.

After the first few times he lined up at cornerback, Benny could tell that Coach Watkins was right. He WAS fast—just like in the sprints he had run that first day—and he could run step-for-step with anyone trying to catch a pass. He learned quickly how to deflect the ball and try to intercept it. He also did a good job tackling. That was a skill he'd never had a chance to work on while he was playing quarterback.

After Wednesday's practice, the coach bragged on Benny in front of the whole team. "With Ben's speed, he can stay with any receiver we'll face this season," the coach said. "That means other teams will have to try to run the ball more, so the rest of us need to work on a run-stopping defense."

Benny couldn't remember the last time anyone had bragged on him. His mom was the only one who never called him stupid or lazy. But she never said anything very good about him, either. She just seemed to feel sorry for him when other people criticized him or made fun of him, and that didn't help his feelings at all.

What his dad had said after the first football game hurt as bad as any spanking Benny ever got.

"What happened out there, son?" his dad had asked on the way home, as Benny slumped in the back seat of the van. "Did you just go totally brain-dead or something?"

Benny had just stared out the side window and didn't answer. His teeth were clenched so hard he thought they were going to break. Why couldn't his dad understand once in a while?

Why did he always have to make Benny feel so miserable, so hopeless?

Just last Saturday, Benny had been ready to give up. But when Coach Watkins bragged on him, it made everything different. The coach's compliments were like a Band-Aid on a cut finger. But deep down inside, Benny could still feel the pain of constant failure.

The week finally ended and Saturday came. The Tigers' opponent today was Collins Elementary, a team Coach Watkins said they could beat. But as Benny rode to the football field with his parents and sister, it was almost as if last Saturday was happening all over again.

"Your pants are still too loose," Maggie said, grinning and popping her chewing gum. "I sure hope you don't make a fool of yourself today."

"Be careful, Benny," his mother said as he got out of the van. "I don't want you to get hurt."

Benny didn't say anything. He just nodded and started jogging toward the north end of the field, where the other Wheeler players were starting their drills.

Benny didn't like riding to the football field with his sister.

"Just remember," his dad called after him, "everybody's going to be watching you, so don't goof up. If you do, I'll never hear the last of it from the other fathers!"

Even the first part of today's game was almost a repeat of last Saturday. The teams battled each other up and down the field, but neither one could score. The first three quarters ended in another 0-0 tie. The main difference this time, though, was that Benny had knocked away the only pass thrown in his direction.

"Congratulations, Ben," the coach had told him at halftime. "You saved a touchdown on that play."

But early in the fourth quarter, one of the Collins running backs broke for a long gain. He shook off several Wheeler tacklers and carried the ball all the way to the Tigers' ten-yard line. It was first down and goal to go for Collins. Everybody on Benny's team looked worried as they lined up for the next play.

Benny watched the wide receiver for Collins as he split out wide to the right. Benny moved quickly toward him, remembering what Coach Watkins had told him on the sideline: "Just stay with your man and make sure he doesn't get behind you!"

Even before the ball was snapped, Benny had a feeling it was going to be a pass play, and he was right. He saw the Collins quarterback dropping back. He saw the wide receiver running full speed down the sideline toward the end zone.

When the quarterback threw the ball, Benny was running stride for stride with the wide receiver. He saw the ball coming toward him in a wobbly spiral. He saw the receiver raise his arms, straining to catch the pass.

For a split-second, all of Benny's doubts and fears came flooding back over him. He and the Collins receiver were almost to the goal line. If the receiver caught the ball, it was a certain touchdown. The whole game was on the line, the same as last week.

"Am I going to mess up again?" Benny wondered. "Am I going to be the goat, just like before?"

Then he heard a quiet voice inside his head, and Coach Watkins' words came back to him: *With Ben's speed, he can stay with any receiver . . . cover him like a blanket.*

At the last possible second, Benny leaped for the ball. The receiver leaped, too, but Benny leaped higher. He felt the ball bounce on the tips of his fingers for an instant. Then he gathered it into his arms. He hugged it tightly against his chest. As he turned back upfield, the Collins receiver tumbled to the ground behind him.

Suddenly there was nothing in front of Benny but green grass and white lines. He could hear the Wheeler fans screaming in the stands as he returned the interception 99 yards for a touchdown. They were the same fans who had groaned in disgust last week, but this time they were all on their feet applauding.

Benny heard cheers as he scored a touchdown.

As he crossed the Collins goal line, Benny felt as if his feet weren't even touching the ground. He seemed to be floating on a cloud as his cheering teammates swarmed over him in the end zone.

A few moments later, the game ended in a 6-0 Wheeler victory. Coach Watkins was wearing a broad smile as he called his victorious players together on the sideline.

"You all played a super game, guys," he said. "You played hard and you played tough. Every one of you had a part in winning this game, and you all deserve to be proud."

Then the coach paused and walked over to Benny. "But I think we all know who deserves the most credit of all," he said, handing Benny the game ball. "Ben Whitley saved the game for us a couple of times with his pass defense. Then he won it for us with that great interception return."

Benny grinned as his teammates slapped him on the shoulder pads and chanted: "Benny, Benny, Benny!"

After the celebration, the other players gradually drifted away. But Benny lingered behind. He had something he wanted to say to

Coach Watkins, but he didn't want to just blurt it out in front of the whole team.

"Thanks, Coach," he said. "Thanks for believing in me."

"You've already given me thanks enough by winning the game, Ben," the coach said. "But the most important thing is that you learned a valuable lesson today. That's even more important than the game itself."

Benny smiled uncertainly. "What kind of lesson, Coach?"

"You learned that one failure doesn't mean you always have to fail. You learned it doesn't matter how many times you fall down. It's how many times you get back up that's important. So don't ever give up on yourself again, OK?"

Benny's smile broadened. "OK, Coach," he promised. "I won't."

Chapter 8

Benny Experiences New Feelings

All that weekend, Benny felt like a winner. It was the best feeling he had ever had. And this time, his family didn't do anything to ruin it. For once, Maggie didn't have a single mean or sarcastic thing to say. Benny's mother baked his favorite chocolate chip cookies for him. And his dad actually gave him a big hug.

"That was a tremendous play, son," his dad beamed. "You won't see a better one in the whole NFL this weekend."

On Sunday, Benny and his dad watched the Dallas Cowboys play the Washington Redskins. And when a Dallas cornerback intercepted a pass and ran it back about forty yards, his dad turned to Benny and grinned.

"There goes my boy," he said. "Only you were better."

"There goes my boy," Benny's dad said.

Chapter 9

Benny Encounters Miss Morrison

Back at school on Monday morning, the good feeling continued—at least at first. As Benny sauntered down the hall, he heard a shout from behind him.

"Hey, Benny, what's going on?"

He turned and saw it was David Newman. David was a teammate and one of the most popular kids in the fifth grade. He had also been one of the first guys to call Benny "stupid." Right now, though, he seemed as friendly as he could be.

"Man, you were really something else Saturday," David said. "Because of you, we've got a good chance to win the city trophy."

"I guess I just happened to be in the right place at the right time," Benny said humbly.

As he walked briskly toward his first class, Benny squared his shoulders and held his head high. He hadn't felt such self-confidence in years. He was proud of what he had done, and he intended to let everybody know it. In just one week, his whole life had changed. He liked being a star. He liked it a lot!

He even flashed a big smile at Miss Morrison, who had been his worst enemy when he was in third grade.

"Morning, Miss Morrison," he said expecting a big compliment for his play on Saturday.

"Hello, Benny," she said. "How are you doing in reading this year?"

"Oh, OK," he said and quickly moved on.

The old battle-ax, he thought. Why did she have to bring that up? Miss Morrison was still treating him like the same old "Stupid Benny." Didn't she know he was a big football hero now? Couldn't she see that everything had changed? Well, so what if she couldn't? As long as the other kids thought he was cool, Benny told himself, he didn't care what she thought.

But as he reached the door of his classroom, he didn't feel nearly as happy as he had a few moments before.

Chapter 10

Benny Loses Hope

At noon, Benny was on his way to the cafeteria when Mrs. Campbell, the school counselor, stopped him in the hallway. "I need to talk to you, Benny," she said. "Could you come to my office for a minute."

"Sure, I guess so." Benny wondered what Mrs. Campbell wanted. Maybe she wanted to congratulate him on winning the game Saturday, he thought. But as soon as he sat down in a chair by her desk, he knew he was wrong. This didn't have anything to do with football.

"Your teachers and I are very concerned about your school work, Benny," Mrs. Campbell said. "You're still struggling in class and having a very hard time with your reading. I'm sure you don't want to fail fifth grade, do you?"

"No, ma'am," Benny said, looking at the floor.

"Then what we need to do is have you evaluated," Mrs. Campbell said.

"But I don't want to be evaluated," Benny snapped. He didn't even know for sure what the word meant, but he didn't like the way it sounded.

"I know you don't," she said. "But it's the best way to find out why you're having trouble. Once we find out what the problem is, we can help you. We really WANT to help you, Benny, and the first step is to have you evaluated."

Benny squirmed in his seat. All he wanted was to get away from Mrs. Campbell and her office. He wanted her to leave him alone. "I'm supposed to be at lunch, Mrs. Campbell," he said. "Can I go now?"

"Yes, Benny, go ahead. But I'm going to have to ask your parents to come in for a conference. Then we can all sit down together and talk about your evaluation."

The next two days were pure torture for Benny. He felt like a prisoner waiting to face the firing squad. Sometimes he wished they would just go ahead and get it over with, but it had to drag on until Wednesday afternoon. This was the earliest time Mrs. Campbell could meet with Benny's parents. Until them, all he could do was sweat.

By Tuesday, everyone at football practice could tell something was bothering Benny. His movements were slow and listless, and his mind seemed to be somewhere else. He got burned by pass receivers three times in a fifteen-minute scrimmage—including one pass that went for a touchdown.

"What's the matter, Ben?" Coach Watkins asked. "Those guys shouldn't be beating you like that. You're not sick, are you?"

"Aw, it's nothing," Benny said, not looking at the coach. "I'm OK."

"No, you're not," the coach said flatly. "You act like you're not trying, and if you're not, you'll end up on the bench Saturday. I don't believe in letting guys play if they don't want to give a hundred percent. Now if something's bugging you, I want to know what it is."

"I'm scared and worried," Benny blurted. "My mom and dad have got to meet with Mrs. Campbell tomorrow afternoon. She says I've got to be evaluated, whatever that means."

The coach put his hand on Benny's shoulder. "Mrs. Campbell's right, Ben," he said softly. You DO need to be evaluated. I know because I went through some of the same stuff you're going through when I was in school."

Benny raised his head and looked at the coach, his eyes wide with amazement. "You did?" he said.

"That's right, I did. That's why I decided to talk to Mrs. Campbell about you." The coach paused for a moment. "You see, I'm the one who suggested the evaluation in the first place, Ben. I know it'll help you if you'll give it a chance. I only wish . . ."

Benny whirled angrily away, not listening to the rest of what the coach was saying. He couldn't believe his own ears. He had trusted Coach Watkins more than he had ever trusted any grownup. Benny had thought the coach was his friend, but now he knew the truth. It was all a lie. The coach was no different from any of the others.

Benny's eyes stung with tears as he dropped his helmet and ran blindly off the practice field. He wanted to keep running forever and never come back.

The coach had betrayed him just like everybody else. The whole world was against him. Everything was hopeless. He would never be anything but "Stupid Benny" as long as he lived!

Angry, Benny stormed off from the coach.

Chapter 11

Benny's Parents Meet Mrs. Campbell

"Thank you for coming," Mrs. Campbell said, ushering Benny's parents into her small office. "Please sit down."

She got a warm handshake and a smile from Benny's mother but only a stiff nod and a sour frown from Mr. Whitley. It was obvious that Benny's dad didn't want to be here, but Mrs. Campbell hoped she could get him to cooperate.

"As you know," she said, "Benny's still having serious trouble in class. He's in the fifth grade now, but it looks as if he's barely reading at a second-grade level. This is very frustrating for Benny, and that only makes the problem worse."

"The boy just needs to apply himself," Benny's father growled. "We're just going to have to make him study harder. That's all it takes."

"Larry, please," Mrs. Whitley said. "Let's listen to Mrs. Campbell. She's only trying to help."

"We don't think it's quite as simple as studying harder, Mr. Whitley," Mrs. Campbell said. "We'd like to give Benny a series of tests to see exactly why he's having these problems. Once we know the cause, then we can help him."

"I think the quicker he takes the tests, the better," Benny's mother said. "How soon can you schedule them?"

"I have an opening Friday afternoon," Mrs. Campbell said. "The tests take about three hours, and Benny would have to miss football practice. Is that all right?"

"No," Benny's father said loudly. "I mean Benny doesn't need testing. I'll see to it that he spends more time hitting the books. I'll make him spend as much time as it takes."

Mrs. Whitley turned to her husband. "Larry, if Benny DOES have a learning problem and you don't let him take the tests, you'll regret it from now on," she said coolly.

Benny's father chewed his lip and shifted in his seat. Then he sighed. "All right," he said.

"He can take your silly tests. But I can tell you right now it's not going to change a thing!"

That night, Benny was in total agreement with his dad.

"I won't take their old test!" he yelled. "I won't! I won't! I don't ever want to go to school again. I hate school!" He ran down the hall to his bedroom and slammed the door as hard as he could.

"I won't take their old test!" Benny yelled.

After giving him a few minutes to calm down, Benny's mom followed him to his room and tapped on the door. She found Benny lying crossways on his bed, staring at the wall.

"Honey, listen to me," she said, easing down beside him. "I want to talk to you."

"No! I'm not going to take those stupid tests."

"Benny, you've been having problems in school for four long years," his mother said quietly. "Maybe these tests can fix all that. Wouldn't you like it if the problems went away and you never had to worry about them again? Wouldn't it be nice if school could be easier and you could learn more?"

"Oh, sure," Benny said. "And it'd be nice if I could fly too."

"There's no reason to dread these tests, Benny," his mom said. "Mrs. Campbell says there's no way you can fail them, so you don't have anything to lose. She says the tests might even be fun."

"She must be crazy!" Benny said. "Tests are NEVER fun."

He turned over and buried his head in his pillow. He didn't want to talk about it anymore. But for a long time after his mother left, Benny lay there in the dark, thinking about what she'd told him.

A test you couldn't fail? Could that be possible?

Chapter 12

Benny's Father Blows Up

Benny was glad there was no football game this weekend for the Wheeler Elementary Tigers. He didn't think he could've played even if there was a game. He hadn't been back to practice since his big blowup with Coach Watkins on Tuesday, so he couldn't have been ready to play anyway.

As far as he was concerned, his brief fling as a football star was history. And he was pretty sure his career as a student was just about over, too.

It had been four days since he had taken the tests, and he was sure he had failed them in spite of what his mother said. When Mrs. Campbell called Benny back into her office that afternoon, he knew the end had come. When he got there, he was shocked to see both his parents sitting on the couch. His mother smiled at him. His father waved halfheartedly.

"Have a seat, Benny," Mrs. Campbell said. She motioned him to a straight-back chair and picked up some papers from her desk. "I've gone over your tests and finished your evaluation, and I've got some good news for you. I know why you're having trouble in school."

Benny squirmed in his chair. He could feel all three of the adults in the room watching him. He didn't know what to say, so he didn't say anything.

"The tests show that you're dyslexic, Benny," Mrs. Campbell said. "Now that we know that, we can do something about it."

Benny's dad looked as if someone had punched him in the stomach. "DYSLEXIC!" he roared. "What does that mean?"

"All it means is that Benny forms words and processes information differently from most people," Mrs. Campbell said. "Ten to fifteen percent of kids are like Benny. They learn in a special way. That's why he's having problems reading. He's being taught the wrong way."

"So, what do we do?" Benny's mom asked. "How does Benny get the right kind of teaching?"

"DYSLEXIC!" Larry Whitley roared.
"What does that mean?"

"That's where the good news comes in," Mrs. Campbell said. "We can improve Benny's reading dramatically by enrolling him in our Resource Class."

The shock on Benny's dad's face had changed to a look of anger. "Now hold on a minute, lady," he said. "I'm not sticking my boy in some 'special' class. He's just fine right where he is."

Mrs. Campbell smiled patiently. "Most parents feel the same way you do at first, Mr. Whitley," she said. "If their child has a learning difference, they see it as a failing. But what lots of people don't understand is that children like Benny are very intelligent and creative. Many people with dyslexia have turned out to be geniuses. Believe me, Mr. Whitley, if you'll give the Resource Class a chance, you'll see a big change in Benny—both in and out of the classroom."

"But I don't want to go to a different class," Benny shouted suddenly. "My friends will laugh at me. They'll think I'm some kind of freak!"

Mrs. Campbell looked silently at Benny for a moment. Then she looked at Benny's mother, then turned to his dad. "Mr. Whitley, it's very important for Benny to be in our Resource Class. You do want Benny to read better, don't you?"

"Well, sure I do, but . . ."

"And wouldn't you like for him to learn faster and not feel under so much pressure and stress?"

"Maybe he needs more pressure instead of less," Benny's dad snapped. "He's not trying hard enough."

"Oh, Larry," Benny's mom said, "I wish you'd stop saying that. That's not what's causing Benny's problems, and you know it."

Mrs. Campbell leaned forward across her desk, her voice wasn't quite so patient anymore. "Mr. Whitley," she said sternly, "I think you need to ask yourself a very important question: Which is more important—your pride or Benny's success?"

Larry Whitley jumped up so abruptly that his chair almost fell over. "Come on, Kathy," he said furiously. "Come on, Benny. I've had enough of this nonsense. We're getting out of here."

Chapter 13

Benny's Father Gets a Surprise Visitor

The next day, Larry Whitley was trying hard to keep his mind on his work. His job as assistant manager of a big distribution center usually demanded all his attention, and today he didn't mind if it did. Today he was glad to be busy training a new employee. He didn't want to think about what had happened yesterday with Mrs. Campbell. He didn't want to think about the argument he had had with his wife last night about Benny's trouble at school.

He and the new man were in the back of the huge warehouse when Larry heard his secretary calling him over the intercom. There was someone in Larry's office waiting to see him.

When he walked to the front of the building, Larry was surprised to see Jack Watkins, Benny's football coach, sitting in the lobby. The distribution center was halfway across town from the school, and Coach Watkins was the last person Larry had expected to drop in for a visit.

"Hello, Coach," he said. "What brings you all the way out here?"

"I think you and I need to talk about something," the coach said.

"Well, sure," Larry said, still confused. "Uh, come on into my office. Does this have something to do with football?"

The coach waited until Larry had closed the office door before he answered. "No," he said, "it's about the Resource Class Mrs. Campbell told you about yesterday. I wanted to ask you to reconsider your decision. Benny needs that class, Mr. Whitley."

Benny's dad frowned. "Look, if you came to pester me about that stupid class, you're wasting your time. Besides, what difference does it make to you? You're Benny's football coach, not his reading teacher."

The coach stared silently at Benny's dad for a moment. "Have you ever tried climbing a hill backwards, Mr. Whitley?" he asked.

Larry laughed sourly. "Of course not. I don't think it can be done."

"That's right, it can't," the coach said. "So why do you keep making Benny do something that's every bit as impossible as that?"

"I don't know what you're talking about."

"Every day when he goes to class, Benny's trying to climb a hill backwards," Coach Watkins said. "He'd do a whole lot better if you'd let him turn around and see where he's going for a change."

"I'm telling you, if he just works harder he'll do OK."

"No, he won't, Mr. Whitley," the coach said. "No amount of hard work is going to solve this problem. Benny's teachers all agree that he IS working hard. But Benny's just like the rest of us. When you keep failing again and again, no matter how hard you try, you eventually give up. That's human nature, isn't it?"

Larry thought about it for a few seconds. "Yeah, I guess that's true," he said.

"Well, that's where Benny is now," said the coach. "Every day he falls a little further behind his class and gets more frustrated. If something doesn't happen to change things, he's going to end up dropping out of school. He'll never get a decent job, and he'll go through life as a failure. Is that what you want for your son, Mr. Whitley?"

Larry sighed and lowered his head into his hands. "No," he said, "of course that's not what I want. I've always wanted Benny to succeed. That's why it hurts so bad to see him like this."

"If you really mean that," the coach said, "you've got to change your own way of thinking. You can't treat Benny like some problem you can solve overnight all by yourself. It's not going to happen that way. It's only going to happen with expert help—the kind the Resource Class can give Benny. What he needs from you right now is encouragement and moral support, not yelling and fussing. He needs you to brag on him a little. He needs you to let him know you love him."

"He knows that."

"Maybe so, but it never hurts to say it."

Larry was suddenly angry again. In the past few days, everybody had started ganging up on him. First Mrs. Campbell. Then Kathy. Now Coach Watkins. Why couldn't they just leave him alone?"

"I don't know why I'm even listening to you," he said loudly. "Benny's my son. How do you know so much about what he needs?"

The coach smiled. "Because I'm dyslexic, too, Mr. Whitley—just like Benny. And you're acting just like my father did when I was a kid. For a long time, he refused to admit that I needed special help. Because of that, I struggled all the way through school. They didn't know nearly as much about dyslexia then as they do now, and most of my teachers just thought I was a stupid troublemaker."

Larry Whitley's mouth dropped open. "But . . . but . . ." he stammered. "But you're a successful, well-educated person. You're a teacher and a coach. That proves somebody with dyslexia can succeed if he wants to."

"Oh, sure," Coach Watkins said sarcastically. "The truth is, I barely made it through high school. Lots of my friends on the football team got scholarships to big universities, but my grades weren't good enough. I had to go to junior college and keep on trying to learn how to read. Finally, somebody recognized my problem and I was able to get some help. But I was still twenty years old before I was able to read a book all the way through. Is that what you want for a bright boy like Benny, Mr. Whitley?"

Benny's father sat speechless for a long time, staring at Coach Watkins and shaking his head. "I never intended to hurt my son," he said finally. "I swear I didn't."

"I never intended to hurt my son,"
Benny's dad told the coach.

"I know you didn't," the coach said. "My father didn't mean to hurt me, either. But he did because he was too stubborn and proud to let me get the help I needed. I lost a lot of time, a lot more than Benny's lost so far. But every day he goes without help is another day lost. Another day he has to make up."

"I guess I've been acting pretty stupid myself," Larry said sadly. "I just didn't realize what I was doing. I'm sorry. You can tell Benny he has my permission to be in the Resource Class."

"It'll be a lot better if you tell him yourself," the coach said.

"OK, I will. I'll tell him tonight. How long do you think it'll take him to catch up?"

"I'm guessing about three years—one year for every year he's behind," he said. "But that means by the time Benny's in junior high, he can be back even with the rest of his class again. And you know what? After that, I think he'll start to move ahead of a lot of them."

As the coach started to leave, Larry stood up and shook his hand. "Thanks, Coach," he said. "You've really opened my eyes. What else can I do to help?"

"Just remember that kids don't fall out of cookie cutters, Mr. Whitley. They're all different, and they need to be treated as individuals. You and Benny will both be happier when you stop comparing him to other children."

After Coach Watkins was gone, Larry sat alone for a long time thinking. He had had a difficult time in school, too. He studied much harder than the other kids, but he always got C's and D's, while they made A's and B's. And Larry's father had always fussed and griped about his low grades, the same way he fussed about Benny's. Larry had never really thought much about this before, but it was true.

Larry had wanted his father's approval more than anything. He had always hoped his father would say something good about him, but he never did. All he ever said was, "You're too lazy. You're not trying."

Because of this, Larry had never gone to college. Instead he had taken a job at the same distribution center where he still worked. He had started out as a forklift driver, but after years of working ten or twelve hours a day, he'd become assistant manager. He made a good living, but he had always felt shortchanged. As a boy, he dreamed of being a doctor, but he'd never come anywhere close to that dream. He'd had to settle for much, much less. It was something that still bothered him at times.

And now, Larry realized, he was treating Benny the same way. He was sowing the same seeds of failure in Benny that his own father had sown in him.

With a feeling of great urgency, Larry picked up the phone from his desk. He dialed the number of Wheeler Elementary and asked for the counselor's office.

"Mrs. Campbell?" he said when he heard her voice on the line. "This is Larry Whitley, and I need to talk to you. I . . . I've changed my mind about that Resource Class of yours."

Chapter 14

Benny's Dad Makes a Big Turnaround

Mrs. Campbell was amazed at Larry Whitley's sudden turnaround. Some parents never changed, no matter how much you reasoned with them. They just went on the same way, in spite of evidence that major damage was being done to their children.

"I'm so glad you came, Mr. Whitley," she said.

"I'm just sorry I've been so thickheaded," he told her. "If Coach Watkins hadn't come to see me, I might never have understood what I was doing. I apologize for the rude way I've behaved. Tell me what I can do to help Benny."

"You can do a lot, Mr. Whitley," she said. "Benny needs to hear positive things about himself, but don't let his dyslexia be an excuse for not doing his best. Instead of emphasizing the negative, you should stress his success—even small ones. With dyslexic children, success breeds more success just as failure breeds more failure."

"I'm sorry I've been so thickheaded," Larry told Mrs. Campbell.

"I can see now why he felt so awful," Benny's dad said. "He was working hard, but I kept telling him he wasn't trying."

Mrs. Campbell nodded. "That's right. Before Benny started to school, you and his mother probably told him all the time how cute and smart he was. But when his learning disability showed up, you started worrying and saying negative things. That's when a dyslexic child starts on a downward spiral."

"You know, this reminds me a lot of when I was in school," Benny's dad said. "I struggled with my grades, too. I'm glad you're going to be able to help Benny. I don't want him to miss out on his dreams like I did."

"None of us is perfect, Mr. Whitley," she said. "The best thing to do now is focus on the good things about Benny instead of his problems. Learn to laugh off his disasters and accept his shortcomings. If you make a mistake or misjudge him, then just apologize. That goes a long way toward showing him your love and support."

"Thanks, Mrs. Campbell," Benny's dad said. "How soon can Benny get enrolled in the Resource Class?"

"Right away," she said. "He may be able to start tomorrow."

"Good," he said. "The sooner the better. I know now that every day counts."

Chapter 15

Benny Becomes a Real Star

Cindy Brennan had been a regular third-grade teacher when she first came to Wheeler Elementary. But during her first two years at the school, she had several pupils in her class who always seemed to lag behind. They did everything they could to keep up with the others, and Cindy did all she could to help them. But nothing seemed to do much good. Then, in working after school with her "slow learners," she began to suspect that many of them were dyslexic.

The next year Cindy decided to be a resource teacher, specializing in dyslexia. Now she spent her school days training dyslexic children who needed a different way to learn. She loved seeing their excitement when they were able to read their first book.

One of her new students this term was Benny Whitley. He came to her each day with assignments his regular teachers had given him, and they worked together on developing his reading skills. When they started, Benny was very self-conscious. Sometimes he got angry and pouted. Other times, he acted silly and tried to distract Cindy. The way he had with his other teachers. Other times, he seemed nervous and overly afraid of doing something wrong.

But as the weeks passed, all this slowly began to change. Benny could understand now that, like all other dyslexic boys and girls, he had trouble connecting sounds to letters. It wasn't that he was reading them wrong, he was just reading the words the way he saw them.

As soon as Benny understood this, he relaxed a little. Learning became easier. A completely "new" Benny began to appear. The "new" Benny made Cindy Brennan smile. He also made her happier than ever that she was a resource teacher.

Benny hadn't liked Miss Brennan at first. He told her so later on, after they got to know each other better. Even after Coach Watkins talked to him about her, Benny wasn't sure she could be trusted. She acted nice enough on the surface, but Benny was afraid she'd turn out like all his other teachers—criticizing him and making him feel stupid.

Only she didn't. Instead she turned out to be more like Coach Watkins. He could tell that Miss Brennan really cared about him. Some of the hours they spent together weren't easy, but she always kept encouraging him. By his sixth week in the Resource Class, Benny felt as if his reading level had jumped a whole year! He felt better about himself.

With Miss Brennan's help,
Benny makes a lot of progress.

The week after he'd stormed away from football practice, Benny went back and apologized to Coach Watkins. Benny finished the football season with nine pass interceptions —four of them for touchdowns. In the last game of the season, he batted down a pass at the goal line in the final seconds to give the Wheeler Tigers the city trophy.

"It was a great feeling, breaking up that pass," he told Miss Brennan the following Monday. Then he grinned. "It felt almost as good as being able to read."

After that, Benny didn't see Coach Watkins much for a while. But one day when he was in the gym shooting baskets, the coach came over and asked how things were going.

"Everything's fine, Coach," Benny said. "I really like Miss Brennan. Because of her—and you—I'm doing a lot better."

"I'm glad to hear it, Ben," the coach said. "You know, it's strange sometimes how things work out. You became a star in football when you switched to cornerback. And now the same thing's happened in your class, too. When you joined the Resource Class, you put yourself in a position to win."

"I guess so," Benny said. "Hey, Coach, did you know that Albert Einstein, the smartest man who ever lived, was dyslexic? And a lot of the other famous inventors and scientists were dyslexic, too."

"That's good to know, Ben," Coach Watkins smiled. "I guess it gives you something to shoot for, doesn't it?"

"Yeah, I can be anything I want to be, Coach."

"What do you want to do when you finish school, Ben?" the coach asked. "Have you ever thought about it?"

"A little," Benny said. "My dad says I can be a doctor some day if I want to."

"Sure you can," Coach Watkins said. "You can be anything you make up your mind to be. But don't forget—the Wheeler Tigers need you at cornerback next year. I hope your career in medicine can wait till after sixth grade."

Benny winked. "Sure, Coach," he said. "Anything for you."

Life at home became a lot more pleasant for Benny, too. His older sister had eased up on her teasing and name-calling. Their dad threatened to take away her phone privileges if she didn't. Maggie had decided to get back at Benny by

"Coach, my dad says I can be a doctor some day if I want to."

ignoring him—which suited Benny just fine.

Sometimes, Benny still resented all the fussing and complaining he had heard from his father for the past four years. But he was also glad not to be hearing the same old gripes anymore. Instead, his dad was actually giving him regular compliments now and even a big hug once in a while.

And one of the best things was that Benny's parents didn't argue about him anymore. They seemed to be united behind him as a team—his team.

By the end of fifth grade, Benny had earned his best grades ever. He had gone from failing or borderline in most subjects to passing with flying colors in all of them. He had long since quit disrupting his classes. And sometimes, he even raised his hand to answer a question. He no longer felt that learning was some mysterious process that he would never master. Now he enjoyed learning new things. His whole outlook had changed.

He wasn't "Stupid Benny" anymore. He would never be "Stupid Benny" again.

When school was dismissed for the summer, Benny's mom and dad were so happy over his progress that they let him choose where he wanted to go on their family vacation.

He picked Disney World.

Epilogue

At the end of Benny's senior year in high school, his classmates voted him "Most Likely to Succeed." He had come a long way from where he started. He attended college on a full athletic scholarship, then went on to medical school.

Cindy Brennan and Jack Watkins were married when Benny was in seventh grade. Cindy still tutors dyslexic children at Wheeler Elementary, and Jack still coaches fifth- and sixth-grade football. Over the years, Jack has turned down a dozen offers to move up to high school coaching. He says he's too old to change jobs now, but his friends think he's still looking for another Benny Whitley. The Wheeler Tigers haven't won the city championship again since Benny left for junior high. Jack and Cindy named their oldest son "Benny," by the way.

When Benny received his M.D. degree, his proud parents attended his graduation ceremonies. When his dad heard the words "Dr. Benjamin Lawrence Whitley" broadcast over the loudspeakers, he cried. After waiting more than fifty years, he had finally seen a Whitley graduate from medical school.

Dr. Whitley is currently doing research in learning disabilities.

# # #

Discussion questions for kids with their parents and/or teachers

1. What does the word dyslexia mean?
2. What does it feel like to learn differently?
3. Can you relate to Benny? How?
4. Can you succeed if you learn differently?
5. As a parent/teacher how can I best demonstrate my support for you?

What To Do Now

If you suspect that your child may have some degree of dyslexia, it is important to have an evaluation to better understand how to overcome the problem. The sooner a child is diagnosed the better, but with the help of a qualified language therapist, it is never too late to become more proficient in reading and spelling.

Steps in Taking Action:

1. A parent, teacher, doctor, or any concerned adult may refer a student for special education services or evaluation. If you suspect your child has a reading problem, write a letter to your school principal describing the reasons for your concerns and requesting assistance or an evaluation.

2. For additional help check the yellow pages of your local telephone book or a nearby metropolitan telephone book under Educational. Typical subcategories are: Diagnosticians, Educational Consultants, or Private Schools that specialize in working with children with learning disabilities such as dyslexia.

3. For more direction use the Resource Section in this book. It contains a list of national and regional associations and organizations that offer a wide range of services for families facing the challenge of dyslexia.

REMEMBER: ***The dyslexic mind doesn't work less, it just works in different ways.***

Quotes From Famous Dyslexics

"Nothing in the world can take
the place of persistence."
Calvin Coolidge

"Without enthusiasm there is no progress in the world."
Woodrow Wilson

"Obstacles cannot crush me; every obstacle yields to stern resolve."
Leonardo da Vinci

"You have to be single-minded."
General George S. Patton

"Only a life lived for others is worth living."
Albert Einstein

"To achieve anything worthwhile you need hard word and stick-to-itiveness."
Thomas Edison

"Never, never, never give up."
Winston Churchill

More Success Stories

Dyslexia is nothing to be ashamed of. Just like Benny, most dyslexics are average or above average in intelligence. Without dyslexia we may not have automobiles, electricity, telephones, Disney World, or movies like *Jaws* and *E.T.*

Hans Christian Anderson
Harry Anderson
Ann Bancroft
Harry Belafonte
Alexander Graham Bell
George Burns
Stephen Cannell
Cher
Agatha Christie
Winston Churchill
Tom Cruise
Leonardo da Vinci
Walt Disney
Dr. Red Duke
Thomas Edison
Albert Einstein
Henry Ford
Danny Glover
Whoopi Goldberg
Bruce Jenner
Magic Johnson
Jay Leno
Greg Louganis
Michelangelo
General George Patton
Nelson Rockefeller
Nolan Ryan
Charles Schwab
Stephen Spielberg
Jackie Stewart
Quentin Tarantino
Woodrow Wilson
Henry Winkler

Resources

National and regional organizations that serve those challenged by dyslexia.

Academic Language Therapists Association (ALTA)
4020 McEwen
Dallas, Texas 75244
972-233-9107

Annual Meeting: April
State Affiliates: No
Local Chapters: No

PURPOSE: A professional association of academic language therapists, trained to help dyslexic children with the basic elements of language.

Academy of Orton-Gillingham Practitioner and Educators
P.O. Box 234
Amenia, NY 12501
914-373-8919

Annual Meeting: November
State Affiliates: No
Local Chapters: No

PURPOSE: Orton-Gillingham trains practitioners and instructors to use the Orton-Gillingham approach to help people who have failed to master the basic elements of language through traditional classroom techniques.

American Psychological Association
750 First Street, NE
Washington, DC 20002-4242
(202) 336-5500
Web site: www.apa.org

Annual Meeting: August
State Affiliates: Yes
Local Chapters: Yes

PURPOSE: Represents psychology in the United States. Works toward the advancement of psychology as a science, a profession, and as a means of promoting human welfare.

Association for Childhood Education International (ACEI)
17904 Georgia Avenue, Suite 215
Olney, MD 20832
800-423-3563
E-mail: aceihq@aol.com

Annual Meeting: April
State Affiliates: Yes
Local Chapters: Yes

PURPOSE: To raise the standards of those actively involved in the care and development of children.

Children and Adults with Attention Deficit Disorders (CHADD)
499 NW 70th Avenue, Suite 308
Plantation, FL 33317
(305) 587-3700
Web site: www.chadd.org/

Annual Meeting: November
State Affiliates: Yes
Local Chapters: Yes

PURPOSE: A not-for-profit organization that promotes a better understanding of attention deficit disorder.

Council for Exceptional Children (CEC)
1920 Association Drive
Reston, VA 22091
703-264-0474
Web site: www.cec.sped.com

Annual meeting: April
State affiliates: Yes
Local Chapters: Yes

PURPOSE: A private, nonprofit membership organization dedicated to improving educational outcomes for individuals with exceptionalities (students with disabilities and/or the gifted).

Council for Learning Disabilities
P.O. Box 40303
Overland Park, KS 66204
913-492-8755

Annual Meeting: October
State Affiliates: Yes
Local Chapters: Yes

PURPOSE: CLD is the only national organization dedicated solely to professionals: teachers, trainers, researchers, diagnosticians, state department personnel, consultants, and special education administrators.

Council of Administrators of Special Education, Inc. (CASE)
615 16th Street, NW
Albuquerque, NM 87104
505-243-7622

Annual Meeting: Varies
State Affiliates: Yes
Local Chapters: Yes

PURPOSE: CASE is a division of Council of Exceptional Children and is a voice for the special education administrator of programs for exceptional children.

The Dyslexic Educational Foundation of America
4181 East 96th Street, Suite 120
Indianapolis, Indiana 46240
317-571-2703

Annual Meeting: No
State Affiliates: No
Local Chapters: No

PURPOSE: A not-for-profit organization dedicated to increasing awareness and support for students with dyslexia, alleviating the frustration and low self-esteem that results from this learning disability.

The International Dyslexia Society
(Formerly The Orton Dyslexia Society)
Chester Bldg., Suite 382
8600 LaSalle Road
Baltimore, MD 21286-2044
410-296-0232
800-ABC-D123
Web site: www.ods@pie.org

Annual Meeting: November
State Affiliates: No
Local Chapters: Yes

PURPOSE: Provides referrals for diagnosis, tutoring, and schooling, as well as information on assistive technologies and emerging educational and medical research. They offer professionals and educators information on multisensory structured language approaches to teaching individuals with dyslexia.

International Multisensory Structured Language Education Council (ISLEC)
1118 Lancaster Drive N.E.
Suite 346
Salem, Oregon 97301-2933
503-363-6891

Annual Meeting: November

State Affiliates: No
Local Chapters: No

PURPOSE: They own and train appropriate training centers for language therapist teachers.

Learning Disabilities Association of America (LDA)
4156 Library Road
Pittsburgh, PA 15234
412-341-1515
Web site: www.ldanatl.org

Annual Meeting: February-March
State Affiliates: Yes
Local Chapters: Yes

PURPOSE: A nonprofit organization that may be the crucial first step for helping a person with a learning disability. LDA has a resource center of over 500 publications for sale in addition to providing a film rental service.

Learning Disabilities Association of Canada
323 Chapel Street, Suite 200
Ottawa, Ontario
Canada K1 7Z2
613-238-5721

Annual Meeting: October (every odd year)
Providence Offices: Yes
Local Chapters: Yes

PURPOSE: To advance the education, employment, social development, legal rights, and general well-being of people with learning disabilities.

Learning Disabilities – Families and Friends, Inc.
P.O. Box 27472
Lansing, Michigan 48909-7472
517-393-5333

Annual Meeting: No
State Affiliates: No
Local Chapters: No

PURPOSE: A nonprofit, tax exempt organization dedicated to providing individuals, families, and friends affected by learning disorders with educational programs and services within a nurturing environment.

The Learning Disabilities Network
72 Sharp Street, Suite A-2
Hingham, MA 02043
617-340-5605

Annual Meeting: March-April
State Affiliates: No
Local Chapters: No

PURPOSE: A nonprofit charitable organization that provides educational support services to individuals with learning disabilities, their families, and professionals. Primarily serves New England area.

National Academy for Child Development
P.O. Box 380
Huntsville, UT 84317-0380
801-621-8606
Web site: macdinfo@nacd.org

Annual Meeting: No
State Affiliates: No
Local Chapters: No

PURPOSE: To help parents teach children with a learning disability in the home.

National Adult Literacy and Learning Disabilities Center
1875 Connecticut Avenue, N.W.
Washington, DC 20009-1202
800-953-2553
E-mail: info@nalldc.aed.org

Annual Meeting: No
State Affiliates: No
Local Chapters: No

PURPOSE: To raise the national awareness about the relationship between adult literacy and learning disabilities, and to help literacy practitioners, policymakers, and researchers better meet the needs of adults with learning disabilities.
Check with your local library for information on adult literacy.

National Association of Private Schools for Exceptional Children (NAPSEC)
1522 K Street, NW, Suite 1032

Washington, DC 20005
202-408-3338

Annual Meeting: January
State Affiliates: Yes
Local Chapters: No

PURPOSE: A nonprofit association dedicated to serving America's special needs children.

National Association of State Directors of Special Education
1800 Diagonal Road, Suite 320
Alexandria, VA 22314
703-519-3800

Annual Meeting: November
State Affiliates: Yes
Local Chapters: Yes

PURPOSE: A not-for-profit corporation that promotes and supports education programs for students with disabilities in the United States and outlying areas.

National Center for Learning Disabilities (NCLD)
381 Park Avenue South
New York, NY 10016
212-545-7510
Web site: www.ncld.org

Annual Meeting: Varies
State Affiliates: No
Local Chapters: No

PURPOSE: National information and referral service. NCLD provides a wide range of programs and services designed to promote better understanding and acceptance of learning disabilities.

National Information Center for Children and Youth with Disabilities (NICHCY)
P.O. Box 1492
Washington, D.C. 20013-1492
800-695-0285 202-884-8200
E-mail: nichy@aed.org
Web site: www.nichy.org

Annual Meeting: No
State Affiliates: No
Local Chapters: No

PURPOSE: Information clearinghouse that provides information on disabilities and disability-related issues. Children and youth with disabilities (birth to age 22) are their special focus.

Phi Delta Kappa
408 N. Union
P.O. Box 789
Bloomington, IN 47402-0789
812-339-1156

Annual Meeting: July
State Affiliates: Yes
Local Chapters: Yes

PURPOSE: A group of professionals that focuses on the promotion and improvement of education, with particular emphasis on publicly supported education.

Recording for the Blind and Dyslexic
20 Roszel Road
Princeton, NJ 08540
800-221-4792
Web site: www.RFBD.org

Annual Meeting: No
State Affiliate: No
Local Chapters: No

PURPOSE: Rents books on tape to members who pay a small annual fee.